The Strong and the Weak: Hammurabi's Code

Tomb Robbers!
A Story of Ancient Egypt

Two Historical Fiction Stories About Early River Civilizations

by Amanda Jenkins
illustrated by David Harrington

Table of Contents

HISTORICAL FICTION

What is historical fiction?

Historical fiction stories take place in the past. Historical fiction stories have characters, settings, and events based on historical facts. The characters can be based on real people or made up. The dialogue is made up. But the information about the time period must be authentic, or factually accurate. The stories explore a conflict, or problem, that a character has with him- or herself, with other characters, or with nature.

What is the purpose of historical fiction?

Historical fiction blends history and fiction into stories that could have actually happened. It adds a human element to history. Readers can learn about the time period: how people lived, what they owned, and even what they ate and wore. Readers can also see how people's problems and feelings have not changed much over time. In addition, historical fiction entertains us as we "escape" into adventures from the past.

How do you read historical fiction?

The title gives you a clue about an important time, place, character, or situation. As you read, note how the characters' lives are the same as and different from people's lives today. Note the main characters' thoughts, feelings, and actions. How do they change from the beginning of the story to the end? Ask yourself, *What moves this character to take action? What can I learn today from his or her struggles long ago?*

Features of Historical Fiction

The characters lived or could have lived in the time and place portrayed.

The story takes place in an authentic historical setting.

The events occurred or could have occurred in the setting.

The dialogue is made up but may be based on letters, a diary, or a report.

The story is told from a first-person or third-person point of view.

At least one character deals with a conflict (self, others, or nature).

Who tells the story in historical fiction?

Authors usually write historical fiction in one of two ways. In the first-person point of view, one of the characters tells the story as it happens to him or her, using words such as **I**, **me**, **my**, **mine**, **we**, **us**, and **our**. In the third-person point of view, a narrator tells the story and refers to the characters using words such as **he**, **him**, and **his**; **she**, **her**, and **hers**; and **their**. The narrator may also refer to the characters by name—for example, "Ditanu felt a twinge of sympathy."

TOOLS FOR READERS AND WRITERS

Oxymorons

An oxymoron is a literary figure of speech usually made up of two words that contradict, or oppose, each other. An oxymoron can be used for a dramatic effect as in the expressions "deafening silence" or "peace force." It may also have a comical, or humorous, effect as in "jumbo shrimp."

Authors use oxymorons as a way to make readers think about the text. When readers find an oxymoron, they should think about why the author chose to use it. Is the author trying to be dramatic, humorous, or sarcastic, or is there some other intention?

Descriptive Language: Adjectives and Adverbs

Authors want readers to see, hear, smell, touch, and taste everything through written words. They also want readers to identify with their characters' actions. To accomplish this task, authors include descriptive language in the form of adjectives and adverbs. Sound, smell, speed, size, and distance adjectives may describe objects and story settings. Adverbs may describe characters' actions by showing how, where, when, and how often things are done.

Compare and Contrast

To add more depth and detail to stories, authors often compare or contrast information. In historical fiction stories, authors might compare or contrast characters or perspectives about certain events, and use the comparisons or contrasts to advance the plot. Many times, authors use signal words and phrases to indicate a comparison (such as *both*, *along with*) or a contrast (such as *however*, *on the other hand*). Other times, authors compare and contrast without using signal words and phrases.

Background on These Stories
Hammurabi's Code

Hammurabi (ha-muh-RAH-bee) was a Babylonian king who ruled most of Mesopotamia (now in large part Iraq) around 1700 B.C.E. He is best known for leaving behind a set of 282 laws, some of the first ever to be written down. One famous stele (STEEL), or stone pillar, engraved with Hammurabi's Code of Laws has lasted through the centuries and was recently discovered by modern archaeologists.

sculpture of King Hammurabi

Writing was a fairly new invention in Hammurabi's time. Instead of pens and paper, scribes (people trained in the art of writing) used the ends of river reeds to press marks into tablets made of clay. This writing system, called cuneiform (kyoo-NEE-ih-form), used pictures and symbols.

Putting laws into writing was an important development for the growth of civilization because it allowed anyone who could read to see what was legal and what was illegal. Imprinting the laws into stone meant that they were permanent and couldn't be changed based on a ruler's whim.

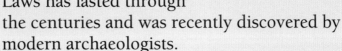

This stone pillar inscribed with Hammurabi's laws was uncovered in Susa, Iran.

The Pyramids of Egypt

Ancient Egyptians believed in life after death and that people needed a large place to hold the things they would need in their next life. Egyptian rulers, called pharaohs (FAIR-oze), built huge stone tombs called pyramids for this purpose. These royal tombs were more than burial places. Part of a pharaoh's spirit was believed to stay with his or her body; the tomb was a shelter for both.

Egyptians also believed that pharaohs continued to watch over their country, guiding their successors from the afterlife. The pharaohs' bodies needed to be embalmed and preserved as mummies. Their spirits also had to be supplied with the same things a person needed in life on Earth. Therefore, a tomb was stocked with food and clothing and also rare and expensive treasures, such as jewelry, furniture, dishes, weapons, precious oils, cosmetics, and plenty of servants in the form of statues.

Putting all those valuables into one place tempted thieves, who risked death to rob the tombs.

The best-known tombs in Egypt are pyramids, and the most famous pyramids are the ones at Giza.

Tomb builders tried to foil thieves by constructing elaborate passageway systems complete with dead ends, filled-in tunnels, and hidden entrances. Still, many tombs were robbed soon after—or perhaps even before—they were sealed shut.

Pharaoh Amenemhet III's tomb is in Hawara, about 50 miles southwest of Cairo, Egypt.

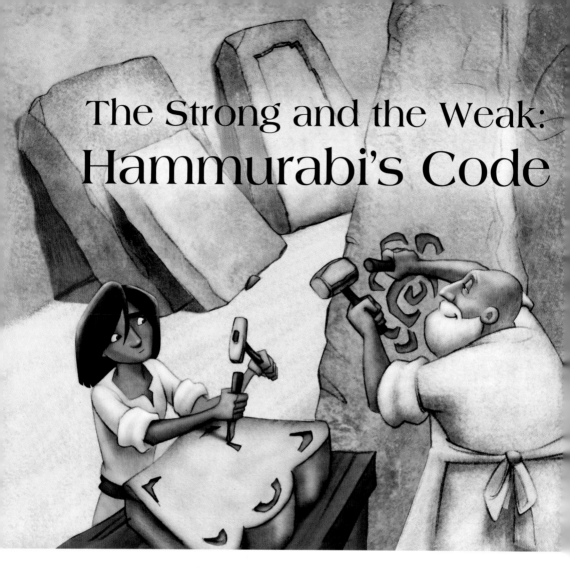

The Strong and the Weak:
Hammurabi's Code

D itanu placed the chisel tip precisely where he wanted it and chipped away a piece of white gypsum. He was carving a plaque, following a pattern his master had created.

His master was Belshunu, a stone carver whose reputation rivaled the great artisans of the temple complex. Five years before, Ditanu had been a ten-year-old waif on the streets of Babylon. Despite Ditanu's unkempt look, Belshunu had seen something in the boy that he could bring out—the same way he was able to see inside a slab of granite before turning it into an object of beauty. Belshunu had offered Ditanu an apprenticeship, as well as a home.

Actually, Ditanu had been living in a home . . . of sorts. It was the home of his uncle Lamusa, a sometime wine merchant, but Ditanu spent as much time as possible outside because Lamusa begrudged him every scrap of food and often raised an angry hand to him.

Ditanu had been overjoyed when Belshunu offered to take him on as an apprentice—and Lamusa was happy to no longer have to feed or clothe the boy.

This morning Ditanu was perfectly happy. A breeze flowed into the workshop from the sun-drenched courtyard, cooling him while he worked. Belshunu was nearby, finishing an important project. The house was roomy, there was plenty to eat, and Belshunu and his wife made cheerful company. The future looked very bright.

"Where is the stonecutter Belshunu?" asked a well-dressed woman as she stormed into the shop, followed by a small crowd of servants. She wore **jingling**, golden jewelry. Ditanu stared in amazement. Wealthy women **usually** stayed at home, delegating any outside business to men or to servants. They **rarely** went parading into craftsmen's workshops.

The Ziggurat (or temple) of Ur, in what is now southern Iraq, is 4,000 years old.

"I'm Belshunu," grunted the stone carver.

"*I* am the Wife of Hudu-libbi," said the woman.

Uh-oh. Ditanu had heard about this grand lady. She was actually a widow; but as was the custom in Mesopotamia, she was called by her dead husband's name. The Wife of Hudu-libbi was known for bickering with craftsmen and bargaining with shopkeepers. No one dared tell the widow of a onetime high-ranking government official that she should stay quietly at home.

"I've heard you're an honest craftsman," she told Belshunu. "I want you to make me a votive figure."

A votive figure was a small statue. Only priests could go into the hearts of temples where gods were worshipped, so wealthy people commissioned little likenesses of themselves to be placed inside. The statues could pray constantly to the gods, bringing blessings to those they represented.

"I'm afraid I'm busy with a royal commission." Belshunu showed her the stele he was working on, a standing stone taller than Belshunu himself. "It's inscribed with King Hammurabi's laws."

"I can see that," the Wife of Hudu-libbi said. "I am able to read."

Belshunu stared at the woman in amazement. Few men could read, and fewer women. Belshunu himself could not, though he had engraved the laws.

A scribe and a court official supervised while he painstakingly copied the marks into the stone.

Belshunu recovered himself. "My apprentice Ditanu will make your votive."

The Wife of Hudu-libbi looked over at the young man, then said, "I have heard that your apprentice is quite the craftsman. . . . He'll do, as long as I get what I pay for."

Ditanu nodded politely, then selected a suitable block of stone. He had made many votives and knew exactly what to do. The hands must be carved in the proper attitude of prayer, and the eyes must be large to gaze upon the statue of the god.

"Bring me something to sit on," the Wife of Hudu-libbi told one of her servants. "I'm going to stay and make sure this boy doesn't try to cheat me."

Ditanu was offended by her mistrust, but said nothing. He just set up the stone and went to work.

His client watched so intently that her **tinkling**, **jangling** jewelry settled into silence. "You've not made a promising beginning," she scolded Ditanu. "In my objective opinion, your work is extremely average."

11

Ditanu paused. "What's wrong?"

"It needs to look more like me."

Ditanu had never heard anyone say such a thing. The gods were not fools. They knew whom a statue was supposed to represent. They didn't need a literal interpretation.

The sooner I am done with this, the better off I will be, he thought as he quickened his pace. Ditanu worked as if his chisel was on fire, flakes of stone flying everywhere. When he was done, he stepped back, praying silently for the Wife of Hudu-libbi's approval so that he could move on to the final polishing.

She looked the statue up and down. "My nose is not that big," she grumbled. "But you have created an adequate likeness, and at least you didn't try to cheat me."

A relieved Ditanu hurried to get sand and a polishing stone. As he rubbed the figure, his client wandered over to Belshunu, who was perfecting Hammurabi's image at the top of the stele.

The Wife of Hudu-libbi studied the words written below the king. "This says the king is the protector of the widow and the orphan," she told Belshunu. "I'm glad to see it carved in stone. Some people will take advantage of anyone they think is weaker. Why, when my husband died, his brother tried to cheat my young sons out of their inheritance. He threw us out of our home! We had to live on the streets until I could get someone at court to hear my case."

Ditanu felt a twinge of sympathy. He hadn't realized the Wife of Hudu-libbi had once lived on the streets.

"I still have nightmares about it," said the elegant woman. "**Sometimes** I wake up in a cold sweat."

Ditanu understood. He still had nightmares about living with Uncle Lamusa and often woke up shaking. He hadn't thought about how difficult it might be to be a widow—even a rich one. What could you do to protect yourself if a man tried to take your house? Nothing—the same way Ditanu hadn't been able to protect himself from his uncle. No wonder the Wife of Hudu-libbi worried about being cheated.

Ditanu felt bad now about doing a hasty job. He took up his chisel again and carefully reduced the size of the votive's nose.

The Wife of Hudu-libbi heard the tapping and whirled around. "What are you doing?" she asked suspiciously.

Ditanu didn't answer. He worked the statue's roughly hewn stumps into feet with individually carved toes; then he engraved lines and zigzags representing the Wife of Hudu-libbi's jewelry.

When he finished, the woman came over and scrutinized the votive figure. Then, to Ditanu's amazement, she *smiled*.

"It's terribly good," the Wife of Hudu-libbi said. "It looks almost entirely like me!" She pulled out a small leather purse; it made a satisfying **clinking** noise when she handed it to Ditanu.

Before he could thank her, Ditanu heard a voice from the courtyard that sent a shiver up his spine. "What perfect timing!" Ditanu felt sick even before he turned around to see his uncle Lamusa.

The disheveled man headed straight to Belshunu. "I've come to take my nephew off your hands," Lamusa said. "I want to relieve you of so heavy a burden."

Ditanu was sure that Lamusa had heard of his growing skill and just wanted the silver that Ditanu's work would bring in.

"Ditanu is no burden," said Belshunu. "He's like a son to me."

Lamusa bared his crooked teeth in a crooked smile. "But he's my flesh and blood. As everyone knows, children belong with their family."

Belshunu gave Ditanu a helpless look. Ditanu's heart sank.

"Come, dear nephew," Lamusa told him. "And bring that pouch of silver with you. Or better yet, give it to me."

"The boy stays here."

Everyone looked around. They had forgotten about the Wife of Hudu-libbi.

Lamusa sneered, as if a dog had tried to speak. "Says who? You? Some nameless woman?"

"The king says." The Wife of Hudu-libbi turned to the stele. She ran a finger along the chiseled words, her bracelets jingling. "Ah, here it is—Law eighty-eight: 'If an artisan has undertaken to rear a child and teaches him his craft, the child cannot be demanded back.'"

Lamusa's eyes widened. He looked up at the towering, gleaming black stone.

"'Hammurabi, the protecting king am I,'" the Wife of Hudu-libbi continued in thunderous tones. "'I have in Babylon set up my precious words, written upon my memorial stone.'"

Lamusa's gaze traveled to the top of the stone pillar, to the scene Belshunu had laboriously carved of King Hammurabi in a

majestic state watched over by Shamash, the god of law and justice.

"You would break Hammurabi's laws and welcome the wrath of the gods?"

Shamash, who sat upright on a throne, looked especially intimidating. Lamusa turned pale under the gaze of the god. He seemed to shrink a little. "I suppose you can keep the boy," he told Belshunu, "if you want him that badly."

Turning away, Lamusa tried to leave with dignity, but Ditanu saw him cast a wary glance back at Shamash.

"It's a good thing you went back to improve your work," Belshunu told Ditanu, who felt like collapsing with relief. "If you hadn't, your client would have been gone long before Lamusa got here."

He was right. Thanks to the Wife of Hudu-libbi, Ditanu now knew that his home and bright future were both carved in stone.

Analyze the Characters, Setting, and Plot

- Who are the characters in the story?
- Where and when does the story take place?
- What problem do the characters face?
- What major events occur in the story?
- How does the time period affect the characters' problem?
- How is the problem solved?

Focus on Comprehension:
Compare and Contrast

- Explain how Belshunu and Uncle Lamusa are different.
- What do Ditanu and the Wife of Hudu-libbi have in common?
- Explain how the first and second attempts that Ditanu makes at the Wife of Hudu-libbi's statue are alike and different.

Analyze the Tools Writers Use: Oxymoron

- On page 9, the author says a well-dressed woman storms into Belshunu's shop "followed by a small crowd of servants." Explain how "small crowd" is an oxymoron.
- On page 11, the Wife of Hudu-libbi tells Ditanu, "In my objective opinion, your work is extremely average." What does the author mean by the oxymoron "objective opinion"? Can an opinion be objective? Explain.
- On page 12, the author says that the gods don't need a literal interpretation. How can an interpretation be literal? Explain your thinking.

Focus on Words: Descriptive Language

Adjectives and adverbs can be organized according to what they describe. Adjectives can describe sound, smell, speed, or size, for example. Adverbs can describe when, how, where, or how often. Make a chart like the one below. Read each descriptive word in the chart. Identify it as either an adjective or an adverb, identify what it describes in the story, and then tell which type of adjective or adverb it is.

Page	Word	Adjective or Adverb	What It Describes	Type of Adjective or Adverb
9	jingling			
9	usually			
9	rarely			
11	tinkling			
11	jangling			
13	sometimes			
13	clinking			

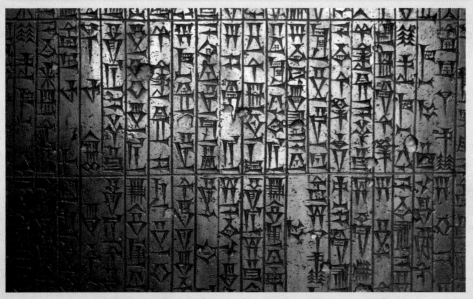

cuneiform writing from the Code of Hammurabi

Tomb Robbers!
A Story of Ancient Egypt

"Mery! Wake up!" Grandmother shook Mery's shoulder. "Hurry! You must go after Khaba!"

Mery opened her eyes, blinking in the dim light. Across the room, her eighteen-year-old brother's sleeping mat was empty.

"He's taken a water skin, a lamp, and some tools," Grandmother wailed. "I think he's on his way to Hawara."

By including details such as "sleeping mat" and "water skin," the author establishes that the story takes place in the past. Hawara is the site of an ancient pyramid.

Mery was immediately on her feet. Just yesterday, tomb robbers had been caught in the pharaoh's pyramid at Hawara. They'd made their way deep inside, opening passages all the way to the burial chamber. The passages would be resealed as soon as the stone workers and masons could be organized. Until then, the pharaoh's funeral treasures were temptingly close to the surface.

Egyptian hieroglyphs carved into stone

Mery pulled her dress over her head and hurried out the door into the crisp night air.

"Catch up to Khaba. Stick to him like a burr!" Grandmother called after her. "Talk some sense into him, and bring him home!"

Mery cut through the village and headed across ripening fields of grain. Khaba had been driving himself and everyone else crazy for weeks. He was in love with a girl named Neferet, who refused to have anything to do with him because he was poor. Khaba had been fretting about how he could get a cow or a bit of copper.

> The author provides a motivation for Khaba's actions.

Mery was soon out of the lush oasis of Faiyûm, and the grass underfoot became bare sand and rock. The pyramid lay ahead, a dark lump against the stars on the horizon.

> The author sets the story in an actual place in Egypt that still exists today. Note that the author further establishes an Egyptian feel with the names of the characters.

When she saw a lone figure striding toward it ahead of her in the moonlight, she started running as fast as she could.

Panting, she caught up to Khaba.

"Go home, Mery," he said.

"I will if you will."

Khaba paused just long enough to grab his sister by the shoulders, turn her around, and shove her toward home. Then he started walking again.

Almost immediately Mery was back at his side. "Khaba, you can't rob the pharaoh's tomb."

"Watch me."

"If you take the pharaoh's treasure, he won't watch over us from the afterlife."

"He's not watching over us anyway. His son keeps raising taxes. Now be quiet, Mery. There may be guards."

They were close enough now to make out the individual blocks of the pyramid. The pale limestone seemed to glow in the moonlight.

"If you're caught," Mery whispered, "you'll be executed."

"I'm not going to get caught," Khaba whispered back.

"Don't worry," Khaba told Mery as he untied the lamp hanging from his belt. "I'm only going to take something small—a bracelet or a vase. I'm not greedy."

The tomb's entrance was a black slit between two **colossal** blocks. Khaba lit the lamp and went in.

The author introduces the problem of the story, which leads to a conflict between brother and sister.

The author uses dialogue to show the potential danger Khaba faces if he is caught and also his attitude toward it.

inside a tomb

Mery took a deep breath and followed. The passage sloped into utter darkness. She got close behind Khaba, and when she nervously took hold of his belt, he didn't protest.

"This is my only choice, Mery," he told her. "You'll understand someday when you're in love."

"I won't be stupid enough to love someone who cares about things more than people."

Historical fiction is set in the past, but the issues and themes still have meaning today.

"Neferet cares about people. She cares about me. She even said she'd marry me if I can get just a little bit rich."

They continued down. **Finally**, the passage ended in a tiny room.

"It's been sealed up already," Mery said.

"No." Khaba lifted his lamp. "Look."

A slab in the ceiling had been shoved back, leaving a rectangular hole.

Khaba handed Mery the lamp, then hoisted himself up into the darkness. When he reached down, Mery considered refusing to give him the lamp. But that would just make Khaba mad, which would only increase his stubbornness.

After he had the lamp, Khaba reached down again. "Come on," he told his little sister. "I'm not leaving you alone in the dark."

Although Khaba is determined to do wrong (steal from the tomb), the author shows that he is really a decent guy.

They headed along a corridor painted with hieroglyphs. Mery took hold of Khaba's belt again, tagging close behind.

"I'll bet those symbols are curses," she remarked.

"Don't say that," Khaba snapped.

She had forgotten how superstitious Khaba was. Deliberately she added, "The priests are sure to have left a terrible curse on anyone who robs the tomb."

"Quit trying to scare me," Khaba said. "It won't work."

The painted corridor dead-ended abruptly. Mery and Khaba both looked up to find another sliding trapdoor, its huge slab already pushed aside. A tense calm filled the room.

Next they made their way down another sloping hallway. This one was shorter and **soon** ended in a chamber with a ceiling of solid stone. Khaba walked along the walls, examining them, but found nothing.

22   **stairway inside a tomb**

Then he looked down. A narrow brick path ran across the floor, leading straight into a wall. Near the wall, some of the bricks had been removed from the path.

"The robbers were digging bricks up when they got caught," Khaba said.

"You mean when the curse took effect," Mery corrected.

Khaba heaved a deep sigh. "*Please* stop saying that." He handed her the lamp and swung the sack off his shoulder.

With a hammer and stone chisel, he began breaking away mortar, loosening bricks one by one and setting them aside.

The air felt like thick soup. It was dreadfully hot. Khaba's tunic was soaked with sweat. Mery hoped Khaba would wear himself out and quit.

"Look," he said suddenly. "The burial chamber must be on the other side." Khaba had removed enough bricks to reveal a trench leading under the wall.

Mery thought he was right about the burial chamber. And at this point, the hole leading to it was big enough for her, but not for Khaba. She decided to scurry through, then come back and tell Khaba the chamber was empty.

As Khaba paused to take a drink from the water skin, Mery grabbed the lamp and climbed down into the trench.

The author develops the plot—and Mery's character. Readers see from her actions that she is not unlike her brother—quite determined, bold, and maybe too impulsive.

Egyptian death mask

The author researched Egyptian pharaohs and is basing this story on a real pharaoh, Amenemhet III, who lived around 1800 B.C.E. He buried his daughter near him in his pyramid at Hawara.

"Hey!" Khaba said, but Mery was already under the wall, pushing the lamp ahead of her.

When she emerged, she was in a room with a **massive** stone sarcophagus. But the sarcophagus was lidless, and she stood amid a litter of smashed slabs and chipped stones. There was no gold here, no jewelry, no vases. The only thing of value was an alabaster bowl lying next to the sarcophagus, or coffin.

Or rather, next to a second sarcophagus. This sarcophagus was much smaller than the first and lay nestled against it.

Now Mery recalled something she'd heard years ago when the pharaoh's daughter Ptahneferu had died. Her grief-stricken father had placed her body in his own tomb, where he would **later** join her.

That meant that tomb robbers weren't taking something just from Amenemhet. They were also stealing from a little girl.

Mery edged closer to the sarcophagi. Both wooden inner coffins had been ripped opened. Inside were two gnarled, **shrunken** bodies. One seemed almost **miniature**, it was so small.

To Mery, the gloomy room suddenly seemed too dark and cramped, the air deathly still. A ghostly voice whispered, *"What do you see?"*

"Augh!" Mery shrieked and almost dropped the lamp. For an endless moment she trembled, waiting to be struck dead.

Nothing happened.

"Mery? What happened? Are you hurt?" said the spirit voice, which she now realized was her brother's! But Khaba sounded strangely resonant and hollow. When he spoke from the other room, the walls somehow twisted his voice and sent it into the burial chamber as an eerie echo.

"I'm fine," she called out. "I'm coming back."

When she crawled out of the trench, Khaba's face was pale and worried. He helped her to her feet and dusted her off.

"I know why there were no guards," Mery told him. "Thieves have already taken all the gold and jewels."

"That can't be." Khaba studied her, frowning. "You're hiding something," he said. He dropped to his knees and began widening the trench.

"Khaba," Mery pleaded, "there's a little girl buried there—the pharaoh's daughter. Please don't steal from her."

sarcophagus

The author gives Mery, and the reader, a good scare. She also sets up a new direction for the plot.

25

an Egyptian figurine

This is the climax, or high point, of the story. Note how the author "pays off" the setup of Mery having experienced the scary echo voice previously.

Khaba shook his head. "I have to do this," he said stubbornly. "For Neferet."

He squeezed through the hole and disappeared, then called out a moment later, "I knew you were hiding something! I can trade this bowl for a cow! Two cows!"

To Mery, Khaba's voice sounded normal. It seemed that the walls only twisted sound going the other way. Mery had an idea.

"I am Princess Ptahneferu," she intoned, feeling a little silly. *"Do not steal from my tomb! "Or . . . the crocodiles shall eat your sweetheart!"*

Inside the burial chamber there was a crash, and Khaba came scrambling out of the trench, empty-handed. "We're getting out of here. Now." He scooped up the tools and water, grabbed Mery's arm, and half-dragged, half-shoved her out of the room.

The next thing Mery knew, they were hurrying over sand and rock toward home.

"What happened?" Mery tried to sound scared.

"The princess's spirit spoke to me." Khaba's voice shook. "She . . . she threatened . . ."

"She threatened Neferet?" Mery supplied.

"No!" Khaba said. "She threatened you."

"Me? She couldn't have!"

"She did! She said that if I stole anything, the crocodiles would eat my sister!"

Mery almost laughed out loud. "Sweetheart,"

she supposed, might have sounded like "sister" in the echo voice.

"It wasn't worth it," Khaba said. "I already almost quit once when you screamed and I didn't know what was wrong. I let you go in there alone, and I couldn't do anything to help. I should have quit then," he said. "But anyway, you're safe now. And I didn't take anything, so the princess won't hurt you."

Mery was surprised to feel tears stinging her eyes. She hadn't realized her brother cared that much about her! "What about Neferet?" she asked.

Khaba shrugged. "I guess she's about to learn that people are more important than things!"

The author provides a satisfying ending on many levels: Mery, the heroine, has saved her brother from wrongdoing; she is touched by his genuine affection for her; and Khaba learns an important lesson as well.

27

Analyze the Characters, Setting, and Plot

- Who are the characters in the story?
- Where and when does the story take place?
- What problems do the characters face?
- What major events occur in the story?
- How does the time period affect the characters' problems?
- How is the main problem solved?

Focus on Comprehension: Compare and Contrast

- Explain how Khaba and Mery are alike and different.
- The air outside and inside the tomb's burial chamber is different. Explain how this difference affects the plot.
- Deep inside the tomb, Mery finds two sarcophagi. Explain how they are alike and different.

Focus on Perspective

Perspective is the way in which people view things or interpret events. A person who is superstitious might break a mirror and assume he or she will have seven years of bad luck. A person who is not superstitious might break the same mirror and say, "Oh well, I broke a mirror." How is a superstitious perspective used in this story? How does this perspective help solve the story's main problem?

Analyze the Tools Writers Use: Oxymoron

- On page 21, Khaba says, "This is my only choice, Mery. You'll understand someday. . . ." A choice indicates more than one option. So what does the author mean by the oxymoron "only choice"?
- On page 22, the author says, "A tense calm filled the room." Explain how calm can seem tense.
- On page 25, the author says, "For an endless moment she trembled, waiting to be struck dead." How can a moment be endless? What does the author mean by this oxymoron?

Focus on Words: Descriptive Language

Adjectives and adverbs can be organized according to what they describe. Adjectives can describe sound, smell, speed, or size, for example. Adverbs can describe when, how, where, or how often. Make a chart like the one below. Read each descriptive word in the chart. Identify it as either an adjective or an adverb, identify what it describes in the story, then tell which type of adjective or adverb it is.

Page	Word	Adjective or Adverb	What It Describes	Type of Adjective or Adverb
20	colossal			
21	finally			
22	soon			
24	massive			
24	later			
25	shrunken			
25	miniature			

hallway inside a tomb

How does an author write
HISTORICAL FICTION?

Reread "Tomb Robbers!" and think about what Amanda Jenkins did to write this story. How did she develop the story? How can you, as a write develop your own historical fiction?

1. Decide on a Time and Place in History

a. Choose a time 30 years ago, 3,000 years ago, or somewhere in between. Set your story in your home country or far away.

b. Learn everything you can about the lives of people who lived in the tim and place you chose so your story details will be authentic. In "Tomb Robbers!" the author researched ancient Egypt in books, on the Interne and by a visit to a museum with Egyptian artifacts.

c. Choose an actual event to rewrite in your own historical fiction story, o create a story based on the life of a historical figure.

Character	Traits	Examples
Khaba	bold; foolhardy; in love; protective	breaks into the tomb to steal a treasure f his girlfriend; is more concerned about hi sister's well-being
Mery	caring; respectful; brave; clever	goes after Khaba as her grandmother tell her to; goes into the dark tomb; goes ahe of Khaba; figures out a way to fool Khaba into not stealing

2. Brainstorm Characters

Writers ask these questions.

- What kind of person will my main character be? What are his or her traits, or qualities?
- What things are important to my main character? What does he or she want?
- What other characters will be important to my story? How will each character help or hinder the main character?
- How will the characters change? What will they learn about life?

3. Brainstorm Plot

Writers ask these questions.

- What are some important incidents that actually occurred in my historical setting? How can I turn one of those real-life experiences into a story?
- What is the main problem, or conflict?
- What events happen?
- How does the story end?
- Will my readers be entertained? Will they learn something?

Setting	The Hawara pyramid in ancient Egypt around 1800 B.C.E.
Problem of the Story	Khaba wants to steal some small object from the pharaoh's tomb to impress his beloved, but his sister, Mery, wants to stop him from committing a crime.
Story Events	1. Grandmother wakes up Mery and tells her to follow Khaba, who is going to steal from the pharaoh's tomb. 2. Mery catches up with Khaba and tries to convince him to not steal; he explains he is doing it for love. 3. Mery goes into the tomb with Khaba. They make their way through eerie passageways and find the burial chamber. 4. Mery squeezes into the chamber ahead of Khaba and finds that it houses sarcophagi for the pharaoh and also his daughter, who died when she was only a little girl. 5. Mery is scared by Khaba calling after her; he sounds ghostly from the other side of the chamber, like a spirit voice. 6. Mery exits the chamber and Khaba goes in; Mery pretends to be a spirit voice threatening harm to Khaba's beloved.
Solution to the Problem	In fear Khaba abandons the treasure, and the two flee. Mery later discovers that Khaba had thought the spirit was targeting *her*, and he had left to protect his sister from harm.

Glossary

clinking   (KLIN-king) making a slight metallic sound (page 13)

colossal   (kuh-LAH-sul) huge; incredibly big (page 20)

finally   (FY-nul-ee) at long last; ultimately (page 21)

jangling   (JAN-guh-ling) giving off a mix of loud, ringing sounds (page 11)

jingling   (JIN-guh-ling) making a light clinking sound (page 9)

later   (LAY-ter) sometime after the stated time (page 24)

massive   (MA-siv) huge (page 24)

miniature   (MIH-nee-uh-cher) much reduced in scale; tiny (page 25)

rarely   (RAIR-lee) seldom (page 9)

shrunken   (SHRUN-ken) smaller in size than before (page 25)

sometimes   (SUM-timez) occasionally (page 13)

soon   (SOON) before long (page 22)

tinkling   (TIN-kuh-ling) making a light ringing noise (page 11)

usually   (YOO-zhuh-wuh-lee) by normal routine or custom (page 9)